Invitations to Personal Reading
Curriculum Foundation Classroom Library
Scott, Foresman and Company

Realistic Stories	
Betsy's Little Star	Carolyn Haywood
Emmett's Pig	Mary Stolz
Mop Top	Don Freeman
Nobody Listens to Andrew	Elizabeth Guilfoile
A Pair of Red Clogs	Masako Matsuno
Animals —True and Imaginary	
Baby Elephant's Trunk	Sesyle Joslin
Little Black Puppy	Charlotte Zolotow
The No-Bark Dog	Stan Williamson
Seven Diving Ducks	Margaret Friskey
The Unhappy Hippopotamus	Nancy Moore
Fun and Fancy	
Four Fur Feet	Margaret Wise Brown
Georgie to the Rescue	Robert Bright
The Mitten	retold by Alvin Tresselt
No Fighting, No Biting!	Else Minarik
The Three Wishes	retold by Joseph Jacobs
Books to Enrich the Content Fields	
The Big Book of Real Building and Wrecking Machines	George Zaffo
Columbus	Ingri and Edgar d'Aulaire
Space Alphabet	Irene Zacks
What Is A Frog	Gene Darby
What's Inside?	May Garelick
Books Too Good to Miss	
Away We Go!	compiled by Catherine McEwen
Hide and Seek Fog	Alvin Tresselt
I Wish, I Wish	Lisl Weil
Inch by Inch	Leo Lionni
Otto in Africa	William Pène du Bois

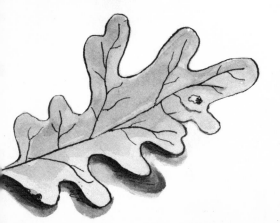

THE THREE WISHES

pictures by Paul Galdone

WHITTLESEY HOUSE · McGRAW-HILL BOOK COMPANY

New York   Toronto   London

Special Scott, Foresman and Company Edition
for the *Invitations to Personal Reading* Program

Library of Congress Catalog Card Number: 61-15909
Published by Whittlesey House,
McGraw-Hill Book Company

Printed in the United States of America

_____

This edition is printed and distributed by Scott, Foresman and
Company by special arrangement with McGraw-Hill Book
Company, a division of McGraw-Hill, Inc., 330 West 42nd
Street, New York, N. Y. 10036.

THE THREE WISHES dates all the way back to Greek mythology
and has appeared in many versions and in many languages.
This telling is from MORE ENGLISH FAIRY TALES, edited by
Joseph Jacobs and reprinted by permission of G. P. Putnam Sons.

To Charlie

nce upon a time, and be sure 't was a long time ago, there lived a poor woodman in a great forest,

and every day of his life he went out
to fell timber.
So one day he started out,
and the goodwife filled his wallet
and slung his bottle on his back,
that he might have meat and drink
in the forest.

He had marked out a huge old oak,
which, thought he, would furnish many
and many a good plank.
And when he was come to it,
he took his axe in his hand
and swung it round his head
as though he were minded
to fell the tree at one stroke.

But he hadn't given one blow,
when what should he hear
but the pitifullest entreating,
and there stood before him a fairy
who prayed and beseeched him
to spare the tree.

He was dazed, as you may fancy,
with wonderment and affright,
and he couldn't open his mouth
to utter a word.
But he found his tongue at last,
and, "Well," said he,
"I'll e'en do as thou wishest."

"You've done better for yourself than you know,"
answered the fairy, "and to show I'm not ungrateful,
I'll grant you your next three wishes,
be they what they may."

And therewith the fairy was no more to be seen,
and the woodman slung his wallet over his shoulder
and his bottle at his side, and off he started home.
But the way was long, and the poor man was regularly dazed
with the wonderful thing that had befallen him,

and when he got home there was nothing in his noddle
but the wish to sit down and rest.
Maybe, too, 't was a trick of the fairy's.
Who can tell?
Anyhow down he sat by the blazing fire,
and as he sat he waxed hungry,
though it was a long way off supper-time yet.

"Hasn't thou naught for supper, dame?"
said he to his wife.
"Nay, not for a couple of hours yet,"
said she.

"Ah!" groaned the woodman, "I wish I'd a good link of black pudding here before me."

No sooner had he said the word,
when clatter, clatter, rustle, rustle,
what should come down the chimney
but a link of the finest black pudding
the heart of man could wish for.

If the woodman stared,
the goodwife stared three times as much.
"What's all this?" says she.

Then all the morning's work came back to the woodman,
and he told his tale right out, from beginning to end,
and as he told it the goodwife glowered and glowered,
and when he had made an end of it she burst out,
"Thou bee'st but a fool, Jan, thou bee'st but a fool,

and I wish the pudding were at thy nose, I do indeed."

And before you could say Jack Robinson,
there the goodman sat
and his nose was the longer
for a noble link of black pudding.

He gave a pull
but it stuck,
and she gave a pull
but it stuck,

and they both pulled
till they had nigh pulled the nose off,
but it stuck and stuck.

"What's to be done now?" said he.

" 'T isn't so very unsightly," said she,
looking hard at him.

Then the woodman saw that if he wished,
he must need wish in a hurry;
and wish he did, that the black pudding
might come off his nose.

Well! there it lay in a dish on the table,
and if the goodman and goodwife
didn't ride in a golden coach, or dress in silk and satin,
why, they had at least as fine a black pudding for their supper
as the heart of man could desire.